Alfie's Secret Dragon

Jacob Carnes and others

ISBN: 979-8-6914-3433-4

Alfie's Secret Dragon

CONTENTS

Acknowledgements i

1: THE DAY ALFIE MET A DRAGON 1

2: THE PIE OF PUDDING LANE 3

3: THE WARMING OF WEAVERTHORPE 4

4: LIGHTNING'S FIRST DAY AT SCHOOL 5

5: THE BULL PEN 7

6: JACOB: LIGHTNING'S BIGGEST FAN 9

7: ALL ABOARD 10

8: IMPORTANT THINGS 12

9: THE VISIBILITY PROBLEM 15

10: GROWING PAINS 17

11: DRAGON SONG 19

12: TAKING THE PLUNGE 23

13: LOFTY MATTERS 25

14: THE MAGNIFICENT MASCOT 28

15: WHAT'S BLACK AND GOLD AND VERY MYSTERIOUS? 32

16: BUSSES AND BOTTOM BURPS 35

17: POO HEAD AND THE COLLAPSING CASTLE 38

18: THE WITCH AND THE STONE CIRCLES 40

19: THE CONUNDRUM 50

EPILOGUE 52

Alfie's Secret Dragon

ACKNOWLEDGMENTS

I would like to thank my family for their help and ideas for writing this book. Writing Alfie and the Dragon helped bring us together during Lockdown and we had loads of fun.

I would also like to say a big big thank you to the NHS for all their help for the country.

I would like to thank Voice Communications for helping get this book published.

1 THE DAY ALFIE MET A DRAGON (BY JACOB, AGED 8)

Once upon a time a boy called Alfie moved into a new house.

Every night when he fell asleep he heard a weird noise from underneath his bed. He thought it was a dream, but he kept hearing the same noise. He was so confused about what he was hearing that one night he decided to look under his bed.

To his surprise he saw a dragon sleeping under his bed. He was startled as he could not believe what he was seeing.

All of a sudden it woke up...

Its eyes were glowing as red as fire. It didn't seem to want to hurt him.

"Are you ok?" Alfie said. The dragon nodded its head. Alfie thought of a name that suited the dragon. He called him LIGHTNING!

He came out from under the bed. He looked cold. He snuggled under the covers and he seemed happy, falling asleep immediately and soon Alfie fell asleep too.

When Alfie woke up Lightning was sitting on the chair by the window. Alfie's mum called him downstairs for breakfast. When Alfie had finished he went upstairs to his bedroom to get dressed. He wanted to make sure Lightning was still there.

Then they played together with Alfie's cars and other stuff.

2 THE PIE OF PUDDING LANE (BY GRANNY, AGED 72 AND GRANDPA, AGED 75)

Now everyone knows that, if a dragon blows really hard, fire bursts out of its mouth and nostrils. But in the past people did not always know this.

Many, many years ago, Lightning's Great, Great, Great-Grandfather, who was called Thunder, went into a bakery in Pudding Lane in London and bought a hot meat pie.

The pie was too hot to eat so Thunder blew on it really hard to cool it. Instead, fire burst out of his mouth and nostrils and burned the pie. Not only that, he set fire to the bakery and burned all of Pudding Lane and half of London.

So Thunder learned that he should only blow fire out of his mouth and nostrils when it was safe to do so.

3 THE WARMING OF WEAVERTHORPE
(BY GRANNY, AGED 72 AND GRANDPA, AGED 75)

Alfie woke up on Sunday morning to find Lightning cuddled up with him in bed. Alfie was worried that his mummy would find Lightning and send him away. But Lightning said, "don't worry Alfie, only children can see me, grown-ups can't see or hear me at all."

As it was Sunday, Alfie had to go to church with Mummy and Daddy. Lightning tagged along too.

The church was really cold, so Lightning, who was under the benches out of sight, blew gently. The heat came out of his nostrils and all of a sudden the church was lovely and warm.

The next day Alfie had to go to school. School was also very cold, so Alfie said to Lightning, "Will you come to school with me today and warm up the classroom? The other children will be really excited to see you. Please will you come?"

"I might come, Alfie," said Lightning, "I just might come."

4 LIGHTNING'S FIRST DAY AT SCHOOL (BY GRANNY, AGED 72 AND GRANDPA, AGED 75)

So, Monday morning, and Alfie again woke up with Lightning cuddled up in his bed. "Come on Lightning," said Alfie, "we need to get ready for school."

"Are you sure it is alright for me to come with you?" asked Lightning, "I may frighten some of your friends."

"I don't think you will," said Alfie, "and I can't wait to show you to my friends Jacob and Joseph."

So Alfie and Lightning went to school together. In the playground, there was uproar when all the children saw Lightning. Some were excited, some were a little scared, but all were absolutely amazed.

"What will the teachers say when they see him?" said Jacob to Alfie. "Don't worry," said Alfie, "The teachers cannot see him because he is invisible to adults."

So Lightning, Alfie, Jacob, Joseph and all the other children went into their classroom. Their teacher, Mrs Beresford, said that she hoped they all had had a nice weekend and then asked them what they wanted to talk about.

"Can we talk about dragons?" asked Joseph. The teacher agreed and asked them what they knew about dragons.

"They breathe fire out of their nostrils," said Jacob.

"They have 4 legs," said Joseph.

"They have long, barbed tails," said Alfie.

"They live under the ocean, but they can fly," said Elsa.

"They are very colourful and red dragons are the strongest," said Daisy.

"Well," said Mrs Beresford, "You are very well informed. How clever you all are." Jacob giggled. "What are you laughing at?" asked Mrs Beresford.

"Well," said Jacob, "We saw a dragon in the playground this morning and he is now sitting on the floor near your desk." All the children laughed!

"Tut, tut, what a lively imagination you have Jacob," said Mrs Beresford. "Now then, it's time to do some reading."

"Can we read about dragons?" asked Joseph.

"No, no," said Mrs Beresford, "We've talked quite enough about dragons for today."

5 THE BULL PEN
(BY GRANDPA, AGED 75 AND MUM, AGED 45)

Alfie had taken Lightning to school and, at lunchtime, Lightning hid under the table, now and again breathing warm air onto Alfie's cold legs.

After lunch, all the children went out to play and the boys started a game of football. Lightning joined in and was really enjoying himself until one of the bigger boys kicked the ball so hard that it hit Lightning and broke his wing.

Alfie was very upset. "What can we do?" he asked.

None of the children had any ideas until Jacob said "I know. My mum is a vet, she will know what to do. I'll go home and ask her to help."

"But she won't be able to help" said Alfie. "Dragons cannot be seen by adults, only by children."

"Well," said Jacob, "I'll ask her how she would mend a bird's broken wing. It will be just the same."

So after school, Jacob ran home and asked his mum. She told Jacob that she would bandage the broken wing with bandaging tape, wrap the broken wing in a towel, keeping the wing held against the bird's body. But she said that it would need to stay wrapped up in a cage for four weeks.

Jacob ran back to tell Alfie what to do. "Well," said Alfie, "We can do all of that, but we don't have a cage big enough for a large dragon."

"I know," said Joseph. "Our bull has just gone to another farm, our pen is free so he could go in there to recover." Alfie thought this was a great idea.

Alfie asked Elsa to help bandage Lightning's wing as she had a special way with animals and he knew she could calm him as they did it.

After Lightning's wing was carefully strapped in place, the children took him to Joseph's farm. It was quite a long walk to the farm and Lightning was too tired after his bandaging to walk (and he couldn't fly!). Freddie, who was the strongest in the class, carried him all the way and placed him carefully in the pen.

"You will have to feed him, Joseph." said Alfie.

"What do you think he will eat?" replied Joseph.

The children tried all types of delicious foods like sausage rolls, iced donuts, and even Haribos but Lightning turned his nose up at them all.

To pass the time whilst they thought of the next thing to try, Izzy and Izabella decided to make a daisy chain with the flowers from Joseph's field. All of a sudden Lightning's ears pricked up, his nostrils flared and his wing flapped (the other was luckily strapped down). Izzy carefully took the daisy chain over to him and held it out. He sucked it up like a length of spaghetti! The children giggled in delight. Who would have thought a dragon ate flowers?!

Joseph said, "Well I'm not picking flowers!"

"Me neither," said Jacob.

"Nor me!" said Freddie.

Izzy, Izabella, Elsa and Daisy sighed, "Don't worry, we will collect the flowers and feed Lightning."

So Lightning had four weeks rest to recover at Joseph's farm. Although, the girls' parents were a little surprised at their daughters' new found hobby of collecting large amounts of daisies, dandelions and buttercups!

6 JACOB: LIGHTNING'S BIGGEST FAN (BY JACOB, AGED 8)

When Lightning could finally leave the bull pen, he flew straight up. But he found he could only fly in circles and not in a straight line.

Alfie said, "Does anyone have an idea how we can help?"

Jacob said, "I do." and ran off home.

The problem was that one wing was now stronger than the other, making him fly in circles.

Jacob came back with a fan and said, "If we point this at his weak wing he can fly against it and his wing will become strong again."

After five days of hard work, his wing was stronger.

Lightning said to the children, "Come on my back and I will take you for a ride."

So all the children jumped on and flew away high into the sky.

7 ALL ABOARD
(BY DAD, AGED 43)

The children, although a little nervous at first, soon relaxed and couldn't believe how high and fast Lightning could fly. They had to hold on really tight, all in a line on a slippery back that wasn't designed for passengers.

When he swooped and looped it was like being on a sky-high fairground ride. Then he darted straight ahead along the Wolds Valley in what they were sure was a Butterwick to West Lutton speed record!

However, during this fearless flight, they also quickly realised that although Lightning was invisible they still were not and for any onlookers it would seem as though a row of children were being reeled in on an extremely long retractable washing line at immense speed.

As they passed over Weaverthorpe Church, Rev Bowden dropped all the hymn books he was carrying in shock and the following rush of wind scattered them across the graveyard.

Luckily for the children they passed so quickly that by the time he had chance to wipe his eyes in disbelief they were gone.

This wasn't the first time his invisibility had nearly got them in to trouble, such as:

• The time he fell asleep on Izzy's feet at lunch and she couldn't leave the table so was late for classes.

- The time he started eating the flowers from their pots in Mrs Beresford's classroom, assuming they were 'mid-morning treats', meaning they 'magically' disappeared one by one during science.

- And don't even mention the time he had a wee on the classroom floor as he has been inside too long. Freddie, thinking quickly, had to take the blame saying he had spilt his water bottle…something that got him a nod of appreciation from his fellow classmates as they all went 'phew.'

Seeing what was happening, and to avoid as much questioning as possible, Elsa, who was holding on to his neck as tightly as possible, whispered in Lightning's ear that he had better return them home going as high as possible to be out of sight of unsuspecting adults.

After Lightning had touched back down (with all the finesse of a ton of bricks – to be fair he wasn't used to the extra weight on landing), and the children had dusted themselves down, they re-grouped.

"It's plain to see that if we don't want to be getting in to trouble, but we do want to be able to fly on Lightning, we need a plan to disguise us when we are riding him," said Jacob.

"Any ideas anyone?"

8 IMPORTANT THINGS
(BY UNCLE STEVE, AGED 49)

It was a wet and miserable Sunday morning in late February. It had been raining for days, and Alfie hadn't played outside for ages. He hadn't been able to think of a way of staying hidden on dragon flights either.

Today, though, he looked especially miserable. He sat by the kitchen window and drew shapes in the condensation with his finger. He drew a house, and a car, and something that looked a bit like a little dog. But after a while they went all dribbly and he wiped them away with the palm of his hand, and watched the raindrops chasing each other down the outside of the glass instead.

"How about I make you some hot chocolate?" said Mum. "That will brighten the morning up."

Alfie thought for a moment then said, "No, thank you Mum, not today." Alfie went back to watching the rain.

Jacob arrived. "Hello Alfie! Shall we play a game?" said Jacob.

"Hm, no, thank you Jacob, not today," said Alfie, whilst he drew another dribbly shape on the window.

Jacob and Alfie's mum looked at one another and shrugged, and Jacob went to watch something on the television for a while, hoping that Alfie would come and join him.

Lightning padded softly up to Alfie and gently nudged his leg with his snout.

"You don't seem very happy today, Alfie," said Lightning. "Is there anything I can do to help?"

Alfie stared out the window for a little while longer then said "Well I was thinking about how grown-ups can't see dragons and trying to think of how I could stay hidden when we go for rides. But then I realised one day that I will be a grown-up and then I won't even be able to see you, let alone ride with you, and that's made me feel very sad."

"Ah," said Lightning, "Well you see it's not quite like that. It's not that grown-ups can't see dragons, it's more that they just don't see dragons."

"What happens is their heads get full up of other things. They start to fuss about whether people will like their hair, or their new jumper or the size of their television. Or they worry about being too fat or too thin, or if their job makes them seem important enough, or if enough people will like their new shoes. And they think that these are important things to have inside their heads."

"And then what happens is the really important things, like being able to remember the smell of a forest after a storm, or to play a game with friends, or to see dragons, fall out of their heads and they forget how to do them."

"Oh!" said Alfie, looking brighter, "So it doesn't have to be like that?" he said.

"Not at all," said Lightning. "You can choose. It takes a bit of practice to remember what important things really are, but it's really not that hard to do."

"Well, that's very good news," said Alfie. "I'll start practicing right now."

"Will it help me become invisible when I ride you?" asked Alfie, looking hopeful.

"No," replied Lightning.

Alfie took a long hard look at Lightning to make sure he really knew what a dragon looked like, then he joined Jacob and played games happily for the rest of the day.

9 THE VISIBILITY PROBLEM
(BY MUM, AGED 45)

At playtime the children were sat on the grass in the playground pondering their invisibility problem.

Lightning was bouncing around and sucking up all the daisies and dandelions that he could find.

Izabella said, "How about we all wear blue clothes and we would be camouflaged against the sky?"

They thought this was a good idea and then it occurred to them that it wasn't often a blue sky in Weaverthorpe. They could just end up looking like flying Smurfs and that would cause more of a problem than a dragon.

The children eventually decided that there was no way to make themselves invisible. So they came up with a different plan. Expanding on Izabella's idea of camouflage, they asked Lightning to blow enough smoke to cover them whilst in the sky. Adults would just look at it as though it was an unusual shaped cloud and not think any more of it.

Panic over.

After school, the children took it in turns to ride Lightning who, like his name, was fast, so fast that when it was Jacob's turn his glasses went flying through the air 0.000001 seconds after take-off!

As usual Jacob couldn't find them, but luckily Elsa's eagle eyes spotted them and found them in the long grass.

10 GROWING PAINS
(BY NANNA, AGED 73 AND GRANDAD, AGED 82)

Alfie woke up feeling uneasy. He had been pondering for some time and thought that the time had come to talk to Lightning.

He popped his head over the bed but Lightning was not there. This was not unusual, as Lightning would from time to time get up early and fly around on his own. Alfie felt disappointed, as he had made up his mind that he really needed to talk to Lightning.

He had been worried for some time that that he was growing and that he would soon become too big for Lightning to carry his weight. This would be dreadful, in fact, a nightmare!

As luck would have it, Lightning arrived back having had a lovely breakfast of fresh buttercups. Alfie got straight to the point.

"Good morning Lightning, did you have a good outing?' said Alfie.

"Yes it was lovely, clear blue sky and hardly a breeze. Would you like a quick outing before school?" replied Lightning.

"Yes, thank you, but before we go I would like to ask you something if you don't mind."

"Feel free."

"Do dragons grow like humans?"

"Well yes, in fact I believe a little faster, why?"

"I have been a bit bothered that as I grow I would become too heavy for you to fly me around"

"Worry not Alfie, I come from a very large breed of dragons. You may not have noticed, that since we have known each other I have already grown."

Alfie felt the relief dropping away from him and could not stop himself from jumping with joy.

"Time for a flight I think," said Lightning.

"Oh yes!" replied Alfie.

11 DRAGON SONG
(BY AUNTIE JANE, AGED 45)

It was time for Alfie's piano lesson. The practice room was right at the back of the school, and was piled from floor to ceiling with yellow wobbling towers of dusty sheet music that smelled of a long time ago.

"I think if you're going to have a nap, Lightning," said Alfie cautiously, "That maybe in the middle of a lot of flammable piles of paper might not be a great idea. You know, just in case…"

"I think you're probably right," agreed Lightning, stifling a little fiery burp, "Better safe than cinders, as they say."

"There's a big room next door where orchestra practices though, there's plenty of room in there for you to have an afternoon nap," suggested Alfie, "But absolutely, definitely don't touch anything!"

"Okay," said Lightning and padded off to the orchestra room. Alfie joined Mrs Stockill at the upright piano and started his lesson.

A few bars into what was supposed to be 'Waltzing Matilda', Mrs Stockill stopped him.

"Alfie, I'm not sure what's going on here… that's not quite right."

"Well I've only been able to learn the A's and B's and C's this week Mrs Stockill, I thought I'd learn those properly first and then do all the D, E, F and G's the next week."

"Hm, that's not really how it works," said Mrs Stockill when suddenly there was a loud TING from next door. Somebody was playing a triangle.

"What was that?" said Mrs Stockill.

"Erm, I think it was…. somebody dropping a spoon?"

"Hm… maybe," said Mrs Stockill, "It is dinner time after all."

"Go from bar nine," said Mrs Stockill, "Let's see if we can put all the notes in this time."

Alfie raised his hands to start playing again, but before his fingers struck the keys, there was a TOOOT from next door.

Mrs Stockill look around. Alfie shifted uncomfortably on the piano stool, trying to make it squeak to cover up the sounds from next door.

"Erm… I think that might have been a … erm, bird flying past very very fast carrying a straw," said Alfie hopefully. It was definitely a flute or a piccolo.

"Hmpf," said Mrs Stockill, "Well, I'm not so sure."

Alfie raised his hands to start when suddenly from next door there were two loud BOOMs. Unmistakably timpani drums.

Alfie quickly stomped his foot on the floor twice "Oh there was a big spider heading towards you Mrs Stockill, but I think I got it!"

"I see," said Mrs Stockill not looking completely convinced.

Then, from next door, there came OOOMPAHPAH oompahpah OOMPAHPAH oompahpah.

Alfie suddenly jumped off the piano stool and started dancing round the practice room singing "Oompah oompah" very loudly.

"What on earth are you doing Alfie?" asked Mrs Stockill.

"Erm, I'm, erm, waltzing like Matilda," said Alfie, not totally convincingly.

"Hmpf," said Mrs Stockill, "I think I'm going to have a look next door."

Mrs Stockill peered into the orchestra room. There was nothing to see. As she turned back to the piano room, a smoke ring floated lazily up out of the tuba.

Lightning grinned sheepishly at Alfie and curled up to sleep until the piano lesson was over.

12 TAKING THE PLUNGE
(BY COUSIN JAMES, AGED 14)

That day after school, Alfie went on a long journey on Lightning's back. He sat there, on the back of the dragon admiring the beautiful sights he passed. While he was looking around he spotted the swimming pool complex.

He asked Lightning to stop so he could go in and play in the pool. On entering the park he smiled at the sight of not only one, but two pools. The first one was a boring swimming pool with nothing in it. The other pool, however, was glorious. It was filled to the brim with many slides, pool toys, watersports and other kids to play with.

When the duo entered the pool, the hundreds of children sat there astonished, Alfie knew he couldn't say the tales of the dragon because then the grown-ups would hear him, so he left Lightning to talk to them. At first the children were surprised but eventually they understood the situation.

After a long play in the pool with Lightning, Alfie decided to have a go on the slides. He had never dared to go on the slides before because they were too big for him to go on, but now he was older and braver. He queued in the line for the slide and waited impatiently for his turn, but when he got to the peak of the slide he started to feel sudden bouts of trepidation.

He wondered what he was doing, the slide looked way too big for him. Alfie wandered to the railing of the bannister and looked down and then changed his mind about going on the slide. He was so high up. He could taste the fear and began to shake. He went to leave but Lightning stopped him and asked him where he was going. Alfie explained that he didn't want to go down the slide as it was too big. Lightning listened understandingly and offered to help him go down. Lightning was going to let Alfie go down with him. Alfie was ecstatic with this proposal and loved the ride. When he got to the bottom of the slide a massive splash appeared at the pool. The grown-ups wondered what it was but Alfie knew it was Lightning.

Alfie thanked Lightning and gave him a big hug. Alfie wanted to have another go on the slide but Lightning said no, it was time to leave and go home before Alfie's parents noticed.

13 LOFTY MATTERS
(BY NANNA, AGED 73 AND GRANDAD, AGED 82)

It was bed time and Alfie had been reading his book and was beginning to feel quite sleepy. He tucked himself under the duvet and was just about to settle down when he realised that Lightning was sat up by his bed and not cuddled up under it.

"Are you alright Lightning?" asked Alfie.

"Yes, and no," replied Lightning. "I do need to speak to you. Do you remember some time ago you were worried that that you would grow to too big for me to carry you?"

"I do, but you told me there would be no problem."

"Well, as far as that is concerned, there isn't. The problem I have now, is a bed problem."

"A bed problem?" said Alfie.

"I am not too sure whether I am getting too big to sleep under your bed or whether the bed has shrunk!"

Alfie jumped out of bed and looked carefully at his bed.

"I don't think the bed has shrunk."

"I thought you would say that," replied Lightning.

Alfie was beginning to feel uneasy. "Oh dear, what should we do?"

"Well, if the bed was made a bit higher then all would be fine. Tell you what, you go to sleep and in the morning maybe you might have an idea."

Alfie went back to bed but he was restless. He needed an idea. Out of nowhere one arrived. He suddenly felt happy and promptly fell asleep.

Alfie was awake early and he woke Lightning up.

"I have a plan but I must speak to mum and dad first."

Lightning was a bit bleary eyed and said "OK," and turned around as best he could and went back to sleep.

Alfie went downstairs.

Mum and Dad had already started breakfast. He got himself a bowl of Fruit and Fibre and slowly began to eat.

Mum noticed he was quieter than usual.

"Feeling OK, Alfie?"

"Yes, thank you, but I do have a problem."

"Oh! So tell us."

"It's my bed."

"Your bed?"

"Yes, I would like one that is higher. Now I am growing up it feels a bit low."

"Really," replied Mum, "I suppose we could get you one at some time."

"It's just that I have been thinking. Grandad and Nanna are arriving next week and I wondered if Grandad could make my bed higher. After all he did make a tractor bed."

"What a clever idea," said Dad.

"Yes, it is," added Mum "I will ask him, so that he can bring the right tools with him."

Alfie shoveled in the last of his breakfast and ran upstairs.

"Wake up, wake up Lightning. I have got it sorted."

Lightning listened carefully to Alfie's plan.

"COOL!" he said.

14 THE MAGNIFICENT MASCOT
(BY AUNTIE EMMA, AGED 48 AND UNCLE IAN, AGED 48)

That weekend, Alfie asked his parents if they could go and watch Scarborough FC. Alfie's Mum and Dad were very perplexed as they all preferred rugby to football, but Alfie was so insistent that they gave in and agreed to take him.

Alfie had a reason for asking – and it was all to do with Lightning. Alfie had seen that the opposition team was Sandringham Dragons and he thought Lightning would find it fun but he could never have predicted just how much fun.

At first when they arrived everything was normal, Alfie, Lightning and Alfie's parents walked to the ground and were surrounded by the thousands of Scarborough fans there to watch the game, they were a sea of red making their way to the Flamingo Land Stadium. Then they started to see some Sandringham fans dressed in navy blue and some of them had flags with dragons on – Lightning was very excited.

A strange thing happens to football fans on Saturday afternoons, instead of their minds been being full of all the important things that adults are meant to think about, they only think about football and nothing else, their mind is completely full of thoughts of their team.

All of the Sandringham fans were thinking about one thing and one thing only – DRAGONS!

As soon as Lightning entered the ground a man ran towards him "Great costume," he said and Lightning didn't understand what he meant. "Our Mascot is sick, can you come and help us?"

Lightning was not used to adults being able to see him so was quite shocked but because the Sandringham players, staff and fans were thinking so much about dragons they could see Lightning.

Lightning was taken to meet the team and then led them out onto the pitch for the start of the game. Alfie was amazed to see Lightning walk out there and waved to him excitedly.

Once the game started the Sandringham fans started chanting:

"DRAGONS are the best!
We will beat the rest,
Gooooooo DRAGONS!"

Lightning was so excited to hear people chanting about him that he ran around and waved to them all, the fans clapped and cheered whenever he went near them. He ran around behind the goal and started doing some cartwheels and jumps.

"That mascot looks like he's flying!" one fan was heard saying.

At half time Lightning was allowed into the clubrooms where there was a huge buffet and Lightning was told to help himself. He avoided the pies – pies were trouble, but he enjoyed several glasses of dandelion and burdock.

After all that sugary drink Lightning was even more energetic in the second half, the Sandringham fans all cheered really loudly and the players were so excited they played even better than before.

At the end of the game the players came to thank Lightning and the manager said to Lightning "You can be our mascot any time you would like, just turn up to our game wearing that costume. We'd love to have you."

"Thank you," said Lightning – whilst thinking this man was very strange talking about costumes.

Alfie was really pleased to see Lightning after the game and they chatted excitedly all the way back to the car.

Alfie's parents couldn't believe how much Alfie had enjoyed the game, he'd been cheering and smiling all afternoon even though Scarborough had lost 8-0.

"Would you like to go again next week Alfie?" they asked.

"No thanks," said Alfie "Maybe next year though."

15 WHAT'S BLACK AND GOLD AND VERY MYSTERIOUS? (BY UNCLE STEVE, AGED 49)

Alfie was drifting off to sleep when there was a loud burp from under the bed, and a burst of flame shot past the edge of the duvet.

"Ahem, sorry!" said Lightning.

"Do be careful please, Mum probably wouldn't like us setting the house on fire very much," said Alfie, and added "And also this is my favourite duvet cover."

"Sorry, I'd better make sure I don't eat marsh-mallows before bedtime," said Lightning, "They make me very burpy."

"Yes, that's a good idea," said Alfie.

"Do all dragons breathe fire?" he asked.

"Red dragons like me do," replied Lightning, "And some of the other Great Dragons as well. Gold and Brass Dragons are fire breathers too. White Dragons breathe ice and Blue ones can breathe electricity. You know sometimes when you see flashes of light up in the clouds when there's a storm? That's blue dragons play fighting."

"Oh...?" started Alfie, "... I thought ..."

Lightning interrupted, "I mean obviously mostly lightning is caused when small positively charged particles get swept up to the top of the cloud and the heavier negative ones go to the bottom and you get a big potential difference in the cloud that ionises the air and causes a massive spark…"

Alife looked blankly at him.

"… but sometimes it's just Blue Dragons play fighting."

"If there are Great Dragons, does that mean there are other kinds too?" asked Alfie.

"Oh yes! There are lots and lots of Small Dragons. There are the Dragons of the Forest and the Meadows. They are usually quite friendly. Then there are the Dragons of the Mountains. And…"

Lightning paused and looked a bit more serious.

"… also the Dragons of the Dark Woods. They are small, but not always so friendly."

Alfie looked worried.

"But don't be frightened," said Lightning, "They don't leave the Dark Woods very often, and I'd look after you if we ever meet any of those."

"Phew!" said Alfie.

"It's quite rare to meet any dragons," continued Lightning, "There's a Nuummite Dragon that might turn up one day."

"A What Dragon?" said Alfie sounding confused, then quickly added, "Hang on, how do you know that?"

"Sometimes you just know things about Dragons," replied Lightning, "For example, when we first met, you chose a name for me… you called me Lightning even though I'm a Red Dragon and not a Blue one. Why did you pick that name for me?"

"Well it's because you can fly very fast of course!" said Alfie.

"Hm. It's true I can fly much faster than most Dragons, but you hadn't seen me fly when you gave my new name."

"Oh," said Alfie, "I hadn't thought of that. But you're right, sometimes you just know things about Dragons."

"But what's a Mnummnumnum…. a Mnoomnmuonmonight Dragon?"

Lightning chuckled. "Nuummite is another name for The Wizard's Stone. It's black and gold and very mysterious. Dragons turn up when it's the right time for them to turn up. So we'll just have to wait and see. But now it's the right time for us both to go to sleep. Goodnight Alfie."

Alife dreamed about little things at the top of clouds and big things at the bottom. Underneath his bed, Lightning snored gently through the night and didn't burp once.

16 BUSSES AND BOTTOM BURPS
(BY MUM, AGED 45)

It was the day of the school trip for years 4, 5 and 6. The school was going to Dalby forest for an activity day.

Alfie wondered how Lightning would cope on the school bus. He had been in a car on short journeys before but a bus full of noisy, excited children could be a bit difficult for him.

The children decided he should fly behind the bus.

All was well until the bus had to stop for traffic lights in the town. Lightning was too busy looking at all the delicious flowers in the florist to notice that the bus had come to a stop.

Alfie, Jacob, Freddie and Joseph were in the back of the bus and witnessed the high speed collision between the bus and a dragon.

Needless to say the bus won.

Lightning was luckily unhurt but he did have to peel his squashed face and pull his legs off the glass one by one. The shock of the impact made Lightning let off his own explosion. A dragon bottom burp is pretty spectacular. This left the boys in fits of laughter especially as it blew the hat off an elderly lady walking her dog on the pavement behind.

They were then told off for by Mrs Beresford for being noisy in the back of the bus.

If only she knew!

When they arrived at Dalby forest the children were set a task.

They were sent off on a foraging treasure hunt to find different kinds of plants. The year group with the most variety would win.

Being the youngest year group on the trip, the children were a bit down about their chances of winning.

Alfie said "Right, what's the plan, what are we going to do?"

Joseph replied, "Well I don't like flowers."

Whilst the boys moaned, Izzy, Izabella, Elsa and Daisy skipped off down the grassy tracks looking for the flowers, Lightning happily bounced along with them.

"Well for a start, let's follow them," said Freddie.

"Ok, let's go," said Jacob.

After using their allotted time the children returned with their collection. They were pretty pleased with themselves and had found that they had really enjoyed the day.

They had collected 15 varieties of different plants. Lightning had of course been 'helping' by sampling them as he followed the children on their task.

When they presented them to Mrs Beresford she counted 15 for year 4, 16 for year 5 and 16 for year 6.

The children of year 4 had missed out by 1!

"Bother," said Alfie.

Just before the result was announced a strange noise came from behind the group of year 4's.

The children looked around, it would seem during his enthusiastic eating, Lightning had sucked a flower up his nose!

It sounded like a combination of an elephant roar, a mouse squeak and a pig snort... it ended with a huge puff of smoke and a flower was propelled out of his nostril and landed near the year 4's pile of plants.

Lightning winked at the children.

Mrs Beresford looked suspiciously at them but re-counted.

It was a draw.

On the way home Lightning decided that he would travel on top of the bus as he was far too full to fly. Alfie smiled to himself as the bus trundled home, he realised that Lightning's over indulgence would mean that tonight the bedroom would be, well let's say...fragrant!

17 POO HEAD AND THE COLLAPSING CASTLE (BY UNCLE STEVE, AGED 49)

Alfie and Lightning were looking at pictures of flags one day.

"Oh look there's a big Red Dragon on the Welsh one – is that you?" asked Alfie.

"Oh no, that Red Dragon has been on the Welsh flag for a very long time, long before I was born," said Lightning. "I might be a Great Dragon, but I'm only a very little one at the moment. I'm only seven-hundred and thirty-four and three quarters dragon years old. I can tell you the story of that dragon though if you like," offered Lightning.

"Yes please!" said Alfie.

Lightning made himself comfortable and cleared his throat. Two little smoke rings popped out his nostrils and floated gently upwards. He began,

"A long time ago, before Wales was Wales, not far from the place that's now called Beddgelert, there was a Celtic King called Vortigen whose land was under attack by the Saxons. He decided to build a castle on a hill called Dinas Emrys to help keep his people safe. His engineers and architects set to work building walls and foundations, but when they returned the following morning, everything had collapsed, and they just found a pile of stones.

No matter what they did during the day, every night everything they'd built fell to ruins. Vortigen called his advisors, who told him that the land must be cursed, and that he should find someone whose parents were not of this world and banish them. Only then would his castle stand.

Vortigen began the search, and soon found an orphan boy who had been brought up by creatures in the forest and had been working clearing out the toilets and stables for Vortigen's army. The soldiers didn't like this boy very much – he was clever and sneaky. They nicknamed him Myrddyn, which meant something like Poo Head. Myrdynn told Vortigen that his advisers were wrong, and that if he looked in the caves beneath Dinas Emrys he would find the real reason that the castle was falling down. He warned Vortigen that white represented the Saxons, and red the Celts. Although he couldn't explain why, Vortigen trusted this strange boy.

When he opened up the caves, he found two huge dragons, one white and one red. Every night the dragons fought, making the hill shudder and turning Vortigen's castle into rubble. Now the cave was open, the Red Dragon chased the White Dragon from the land, and returned to sleep in the cave. Vortigen built his castle, and the Saxons were defeated. That's how the Red Dragon became the symbol for the Welsh flag."

"Thank you, that's a great story," said Alfie. "What happened to Myrddyn in the end?" asked Alfie.

"Ah, well he turned out to be one of the wisest and powerful wizards ever known," replied Lightning. "Myrddyn was his Welsh name of course. In English you'd call him Merlin, but that's a whole other story."

18 THE WITCH AND THE STONE CIRCLES (BY COUSIN LEWIS, AGED 26 AND BETH, AGED 30)

PART ONE: TO HARWOOD DALE!

Alfie listened to Lightning's story, wide-eyed.

"A whole other story, Lightning?" cried Alfie, "Oh wow, please tell it to me, Lightning."

The dragon sighed a dragon-sized sigh. "Now? Alfie, I'm pretty tired from telling the first one. Maybe after a little snooze."

Lightning closed his eyes and rested his head on his big front claws and after a while he was snoring away, little puffs of smoke issuing from his nostrils after every fifth snore. Alfie was a bit disappointed, but after all, Lightning's story had involved remembering a lot of big weirdly-spelled names; even a dragon would be tired after that.

Alfie turned back to looking at his Great Big Book of Flags, but after a while he was sleepy too. Flags without dragons aren't really that interesting.

"Maybe I'll just have a little nap as well," Alfie decided, and he curled up on the sofa cushions next to Lightning.

Half an hour later Lightning awoke with a start and bellowed "I know!"

Alfie jumped out of his skin and promptly fell off the sofa. Dazed from the sudden rude interruption of his nap, he rubbed sleep out of his eyes and grumbled, "What?"

Lightning's eyes were alight with excitement, "You wanted to hear the story about Myrddyn, yes?"

"Yes," said Alfie, more awake now it seemed Lightning was happy to entertain him some more.

"So, what's even better than hearing a story?" asked Lightning.

Alfie thought for a minute. "I don't know, birthday cake?"

"Well, yes," agreed Lightning, "but even better than birthday cake and even birthdays?"

Alfie shrugged. Something better than birthdays and birthday cake was pretty hard to imagine.

Lightning chuckled, "Why, being in the story itself of course!" And he blew a small flame out of his left nostril in excitement and Alfie had to duck to avoid the right side of his hair becoming slightly singed.

Alfie looked perplexed- once he had recovered from the inconvenience of nearly being set on fire. "What do you mean Lightning?"

Lightning's eyes gleamed red. "There's another secret about dragons I haven't told you yet, because it's a pretty big secret and most humans can't be trusted with it. I had to make sure you were definitely one of the Good Ones."

Alfie was now indignant, "Of course I'm one of the Good Ones –" the dragon held up a claw to shush Alfie and continued: "So now I know you are definitely one of the Good Ones, I can tell you." Lightning paused a big pause and Alfie held his breath.

"Dragons can go back in time!"

"GO BACK IN TIME?!?!" Alfie fell off the sofa again in shock.

"Yes. But you mustn't exclaim such things so loudly – it is a secret after all, and a very large one at that."

"Hm, does that mean we can meet the other dragon... what's his name – mid-errr-rin?" an intrigued Alfie whispered hesitantly.

"Well... perhaps."

"Perhaps?"

"Time is a complicated thing, Alfie, it never really lets you do what you want with it. It just depends how it is feeling that day," Lightning explained confidently. "Now, I want to be absolutely clear that you are sure you definitely most positively want to do this because it may possibly be ever so slightly dangerous annddddd - and this is important - there was a very wise witch in a place very far away that said such things shouldn't be messed with."

"YES I DEFINITELY MOST POSITIVELY DEFINITELY DO!"

Alfie jumped up and down on his bed ecstatically and completely ignoring the idea that such things shouldn't be messed with, "But... Lightning – How?"

"That's quite simple. The stones," said Lightning nonchalantly.

"Mnoomnmuonmonight?" puzzled Alfie.

"Ha! No, no - nothing like that. These are a very different type of stone. They are, on their own, quite everyday stones. Much bigger than a wizard stone, and much heavier. It's how you arrange them that makes them special."

"Well, how do you arrange them?"

"In no particular order is usually fine; would you like to see what they look like?"

And before Alfie could even answer, Lightning started to draw long puffs of smoke from his snout. Alfie's eyes widened as he started to see the smoke form into a shape, and a shape he recognised at that.

"Stonehenge!"

"That's right! Except there isn't much point of going there. There is a stone circle much closer to where we are now. There's one in Harwood Dale, which is only a 10 minute fly, tops," Lightning winked and bowed his head down for Alfie to climb on.

And off they went…

PART TWO: TERRIBLE SHENANIGANS

Lightening soared through the air as Alfie gripped tightly to his mane.

"Can you see the circle?" Lightning shouted as he pointed his claw at the stone circles.

"Is that it? They're a lot smaller than I imagined," replied a slightly disappointed Alfie.

"They don't need to be that big - as long as I can fit through them. Now hold on tight!" Lightning powered upwards into the air and immediately plummeted straight down, starting to chant an old, old language. The stones started to glow and a portal appeared, swirling deep with black and purple. Before Alfie even had the chance to notice what was happening they had smashed through the portal and were soaring upwards into the air.

Lightning started to fly forward. In the distance they could see a large group of people surrounding a fire. The people were throwing stones into the fire and shouting lots of bad, bad words (words which we will not repeat here).

In the middle of the fire was a woman who was tied to a big tree trunk. She stood with her chin held high with pride. Alfie was horrified at the sight and Lightning could sense this at once. The dragon turned sharply and made a beeline towards the fire. The watching crowd began to scream and run in all directions as they saw the mighty beast coming towards them. Lightning landed next to the fire with a big WHOOOSHHHH, knocking over several people who had been either too brave or too stupid to move. He began to slowly gulp inside his throat, a deep guttural, ancient sound. Then he belched a mighty burp, knocking over all the rest of people onto the ground, even those who had been running away and were several streets

43

along – but more importantly - he put out the fire! The startled people all scrambled up and ran away - as fast as lightning.

Lightning gently broke the ropes binding the woman and picked her up with one of his huge claws, and set her down next to the smoldering pile of wood and charcoal which a moment ago had been aflame.

"Thank you," said the witch. "You saved my life. I owe you. "Come with me and I'll cook the young lad something special right up, and I'll make you a brew you'll simply not be able to resist," cackled the woman insistently.

Alfie's stomach rumbled; this was definitely a good idea. Despite her constant cackling, the woman had a pleasant aura about her. However, Lightning was not so sure, and didn't trust her.

Dragons and Witches had a long history – some good – some bad – but mostly bad. On this occasion, he saw no harm in indulging the Witch, so Lightning nodded at the Witch and she made a high-pitched noise of triumph as she trooped away without a word, assuming they would follow in her wake.

They walked through beautiful woods, the likes of which Alfie had never seen, carpeted with all colours of moss, the branches of the trees above making a patchwork blanket out of the sky. Finally, they arrived at a small cottage. Surrounding it was a large garden adorned with every herb and flower you could possibly imagine. Various animals were kept with their own barn - pigs, sheep, ocelots – to name a few, allowed to go inside and out as they pleased. At the gate sat a fat black cat waiting for her owner to come back.

"Come on Tibbles! What have I told you about waiting around for me like this! You're your own cat you know!"

"Meow," and the cat moved ahead of them to the cottage as the Witch picked some herbs and flower heads as she walked along the stone pathway and creaked open the wooden doors. The Witch in front of the open doorway with her hands on her hips.

"Now then!" She stated, "1447! And it's a beautiful year to find yourself don't you think?"

"Whoaaaa!" exclaimed Alfie.

"Yes 'Whoaaaaa!' indeed little one. You should drink this, it's very good for you." The witch offered Alfie a honey-coloured swirling drink in a pewter flagon. It seemed to whisper to him... but Alfie decided it was just his imagination. It smelled so sweet, and Alfie reached out his hand to take it...

Suddenly, Lightening swung Alfie onto his back and swooped up out of the forest and into the air.

"See you soon!" hollered the Witch, grinning as she waved them goodbye.

"What's wrong?" exclaimed Alfie.

"We're leaving," muttered Lightning, "I have a bad feeling about this place... something doesn't sit quite right in my stomach and I can't quite put my tongue on it. I don't want to put you in any danger."

Alfie could see the stone circles now, except this time they looked much larger and far more imposing. They were truly a sight to behold. Much like before Lightening darted downwards into the portal as it crackled open from beneath the soil. Only this time it didn't appear to swirl as fluidly as before. In fact, the portal appeared to be closing rapidly, and would be gone before Lightning would have the chance to reach it – but he wasn't slowing down.

'Is this the end?' thought Alfie. I guess at least I got to have all these adventures with a Dragon, I bet no other kids get to do that. But is this really the end?

Lightning as we know is particularly fast, but as well as being very fast he also had incredible reflexes. There was a large thudding sound and Lightning smashed onto the ground. Alfie fell forward but Lighning was able to land perfectly on his two front arms with his tail poised ready to move. As Alfie started to fall forward from the momentum, Lightning was able to manoeuvre him with his tail, downwards, then upwards, flailing back into the air like coming back up from a bungee jump. Then Lightning thrust himself back into the air and caught Alfie safely in his claws, just before Alfie would've hit the ground. This is exactly the kind of thing Lightning was built for. Alfie was pretty shocked still being alive, but pretty happy considering a moment ago he was facing imminent death in the eye.

"Are you okay, Alfie? I'm sorry that that happened..." said a crestfallen

Lightning.

"Yeah I'm okay." Alfie brushed himself down as he stood up and smiled at Lightning, "That was actually quite fun – can we do it again?"

"Ha, not any time soon. But it appears we are somewhat stuck… and right now I'm not entirely sure what we should do or how we should get back…"

The usually confident dragon looked nonplussed. "Oh dear this is quite the conundrum!"

Alfie thought for a moment then tentatively suggested - though we should point out he was thinking with his stomach rather than his brain, which is easily done - "We could go back to the Witch's? She did seem really nice and I am quite hungry…"

Lightning stared a hard stare at Alfie, and for a moment Alfie thought he had definitely said the wrong thing. However, Lightning eventually sighed, a spark from a nostril setting a small nearby shrub on fire, and lifted Alfie back onto his scaly shoulders.

And back they went…

PART THREE: THE WITCH

Inside the Witch's cottage was a simple bed, various crockery dotted about the wall, an old stove with a teapot sitting on top and a large black cauldron hanging below the chimney piece. The Witch started to throw herbs and numerous unidentifiable bits and bobs into the cauldron, and proceeded to excitedly brew the kettle. The cat stared at her and meowed.

"I know, I know, Tibbles, they're coming back aren't they? Why don't you open the door for me?"

Tibbles leapt down from the counter and proceeded to pad up to the door, pushing it open with his head. Lightning and Alfie had just that second landed on the doorstep.

The Witch didn't look up from the cauldron, "Aha, I knew you'd be back! Now then, I've cooked up some food for you real good and I still have some of that drink I offered you before." The Witch handed a cup toward Alfie.

"Thanks, erm… what should we call you? And what's the drink?" Alfie looked at his cup again, but this drink was a pale brown colour with a flower petal floating on top, and no voices to be heard at all. Alfie shook his head – he must have imagined it before…

"You may be somewhat further in history than me young lad, but surely… surely they must still have tea! Yes, yes I'm sure they do -- now then what should I call you both by? I go by the name Margaret Douglas, but you can simply call me Granny. Now come in, come in."

Alfie took the mug and walked inside. As he gazed around inside the old cottage Lightning stuck his head through the window and puffed some black smoke out of his nose in what appeared to be protest.

"I'm Alfie and this is my friend Lightning. "Can you get us home?" asked Alfie.

Granny Douglas poured some of the cauldron liquid into a bowl for Alfie and gestured for him to have it. This was the same golden honey liquid as before!

"This is the best soup you'll ever have I'd wager. You're a very brave young man, y'know? To ride on a Dragon's back and save an old hag like myself," cackled the Witch. "Don't you worry little one – I know just the trick." She reached down from underneath her bed and placed a wooden box in front of Alfie. The box had beautiful carvings which seemed to glow.

"Well go on – open it," said the Witch encouragingly.

Alfie prised it open, half closing his eyes in case something terrible was about to jump out at him. But instead, inside was a dark oval-shaped gem, swirling with all the colours under the sun and whispering with the same voices as before.

"It's no use to me anymore," sighed the Witch. "I'm old y'see, I ain't got anywhere t'be anymore, and if I do I already know where it is. I think you and the likes of your Dragon friend ought to find much more use for it now."

Alfie looked at the Witch blankly. The Witch picked up the stone and dropped it into the cauldron, stirred the pot and threw her wrinkled head back as she called for Lightning. After a moment the grumpy Dragon stuck his head back through the window.

"Alfie," he began to grumble, "You know when I said such things shouldn't be messed with, I think that maybe such things shouldn't be messed with and…"

"Oh shush your mush!" said Granny, "Don't you worry yourself and have some food."

Begrudgingly Lightning quieted himself, picked up the cauldron and started to gulp down the soup. It was the most delicious thing he had ever tasted and he felt a powerful energy flow into his essence. He instantly knew what this meant.

"If I ever!" exclaimed Lightning excitedly. "Never in my life time would have thought such a thing possible, especially of a human. I can only thank you from the bottom of my heart. I will forever be in your debt, Margaret Douglas."

"No no, there are no debts. I did say that I owe you, remember? This is my payment."

"What, what? What is it!?" pressed an astonished Alfie.

Lightning smiled, "It looks like the Witch has given us a way home. And the Dragon's smile spread so wide that Alfie could count every single one of his sharp pearly white Dragon's teeth.

Lightening and Alfie bid their farewells to the Witch and thanked her for the food and drink and especially for giving them a way to get home. She waved them off with an almighty cackle as Lightning's wings beat into the air, causing the Witch's hat to fall off.

Before Alfie knew it they were back in his bedroom.

"I think it might be time for a snooze," yawned Lightning, "But not before we eat some birthday cake – and I ask you a question."

Alfie was already eating birthday cake. Through his mouthful of crumbs and jam, he mumbled, "What's that?"

The dragon smiled a knowing smile, "There's a valuable lesson to be learned from all this – what do you think it is?"

Alfie paused and swallowed his cake, "Hmmm… is it that your pride leads you to make poor decisions?"

"HA HAAAAAA," roared Lightning, "You almost have as keen an eye as that Witch – but of course you do – that's why I like you. You're right Alfie, today you saw a side of me that I'm not too fond of, a negativity that comes from my own prejudice and past experiences.

"Yes, you have been acting quite grumpy today!" agreed Alfie.

"Yes, that was my pride talking – but most importantly it's that I needed help – we both needed help. It just goes to show that even the strongest of people need help every now and again, even from the unlikeliest of people. I mean a witch!"

Alfie detected a note of stiffness still in the dragon's tone. Lightning continued, "But there's absolutely no shame in accepting that. Anyway…" Lightning yawned the biggest yawn of the day, "How about that snooze?"

And in a second, Lightning was snoring away under Alfie's bed.

19 THE CONUNDRUM
(BY MUM, AGED 45)

After all the adventures the children had with Lightning, there was still one mystery…

Where had Lightning come from?

One night Alfie woke up, Lightning was fast asleep under the bed as usual and a thought crossed Alfie's mind.

He jumped out of bed and started to sort out all the mess of books, smelly socks, Lego and other toys out from under the bed, being careful not to wake Lightning.

He eventually found what he was looking for. Small bits of blue shiny shell in-between the chaos of his toys.

As a result he sat there and pondered the old conundrum, what came first, The Dragon or The Egg!

The End

EPILOGUE
(BY GRANDAD, AGED 75)

Flying Dragons

So that was the story of a dragon called Lightning,
Who came to Weaverthorpe and was not at all frightening.

He became a friend of the children at school,
Who thought that a dragon was rather cool.

So they all had adventures flying around,
Flying so high, way off the ground.

Swooping and diving and frightening birds,
A fiery red dragon with very few words.

But he became a hero to the children at school,
Joining in games and playing the fool.

No-one had seen a dragon of course,
Only a pig, sheep, cow and a horse.

But never, no never, a red dragon in flight,
It really had been a wonderful sight.

It was left to Alfie to say the last word,
It was just a whisper but everyone heard....

"I've often seen a dragonfly, but I've never seen a Dragon fly."

Printed in Great Britain
by Amazon